MINNA NEEDS REHEARSAL SPACE

DORTHE NORS was born in 1970 and is one of the most original voices in contemporary Danish literature. She holds a degree in literature and art history from Aarhus University and has published four novels so far, including *Mirror, Shoulder, Signal* – which was shortlisted for The Man Booker International Prize, as well as the novella *Minna Needs Rehearsal Space*, and a collection of short stories, *Karate Chop*. Nors's short stories have appeared in numerous publications, including *Harper's Magazine* and the *Boston Review*, and she is the first Danish writer ever to have a story published in the *New Yorker*. In 2014, *Karate Chop* won the prestigious P.O. Enquist Literary Prize. *Mirror, Shoulder, Signal* and *Karate Chop* are also published by Pushkin Press.

Translated from the Danish
by **MISHA HOEKSTRA**

PUSHKIN PRESS

Pushkin Press
71–75 Shelton Street, London WC2H 9JQ

This edition first published in 2017

Published by agreement with Ahlander Agency

Minna Needs Rehearsal Space was first published as
Minna Mangler et Øvelokale in Denmark in 2013

First published by Pushkin Press in 2015

DANISH ARTS FOUNDATION

Grateful acknowledgment is made to the Danish Arts Council
and its Committee for Literary Project Funding and the Danish
Arts Agency for support in the writing and translation of the
book – and to Hald Hovedgaard for a writing residency.

1 3 5 7 9 10 8 6 4 2

ISBN 978 1 782274 34 6

Set in Sabon Monotype by Tetragon, London

Printed by CPI Group (UK) Ltd, Croydon CR0 4YY

www.pushkinpress.com

DORTHE NORS
MINNA NEEDS
REHEARSAL
SPACE

MINNA INTRODUCES HERSELF.

Minna is on Facebook.
Minna isn't a day over forty.
Minna is a composer.
Minna can play four instruments.
Minna's lost her rehearsal space.
Minna lives in Amager.
Minna spends her days in the Royal Library.
Minna has to work without noise.
Minna's working on a paper sonata.
The paper sonata consists of tonal rows.
Minna writes soundless music.
Minna is a tad avant-garde.
Minna has a tough time explaining the idea to people.
Minna wants to have sound with the music – no,
Minna just wants to have sound.
Minna wants to have Lars.
Minna's in love with Lars.
Lars used to really like Minna.
Minna doesn't dare click on the relationship app.
Lars has a full beard.
Lars has light-colored curls.
Lars works for the paper.
Lars is a network person.
Lars is Lars, Minna thinks, fumbling with the duvet cover.

It's morning.
Lars has left again.
Lars is always in a hurry to get out of bed.
The bed is a snug nest.
Minna's lying in it, but
Lars is on his bike and gone.
Lars bikes as hard as he can in the direction of City Hall Square.
Lars makes the pigeons rise.
Lars has deadlines.
Minna has an itch on her face.
Minna goes out to the bathroom to check.
Lars has kissed her.
Minna doesn't look like who she looked like when she made the spaghetti last night.
Minna looks like someone who drank all the wine herself.
Minna walks around in bare feet.
The flat is full of notes.
Bach stands in the window.
Brahms stands on the coffee table.
The flat's too small for a piano, but
A woman should have room for a flute.
A woman should have room for a flute, a triangle, and a guitar.
Minna takes out the guitar.
Minna plays something baroque.
Minna plays as quietly as possible.
The neighbor bangs on the wall with his sandals.
Minna needs a rehearsal space.
Minna needs security in her existence.
Minna misses the volume.
Minna misses a healthier alternative.

Minna wants to devote herself to ecology.
Minna wants to involve a kid in it.
Minna wants to try to be just like the rest.
Lars ought to help her but
Lars uses condoms.
Lars is on his bike and gone.
Lars is Lars.

*

Minna calls Lars.
Minna calls Lars until he picks up the phone.
Minna and Lars have discussed this before.
Lars has a cousin.
The cousin's name is Tim.
Tim knows of a rehearsal space in Kastrup.
The rehearsal space is close to the airport.
The rehearsal space is cheap.
Minna's never met Tim.
Minna is in many ways desperate.
Minna says, *I cannot keep on being quiet.*
Minna says, *I've got to be able to turn myself up and down.*
Lars sighs.
Minna says, *Let's bike out to the rehearsal space.*
Lars doesn't want to.
Lars is a culture reporter.
Lars and Minna met at a reception.
Lars introduced himself with his full name.
Minna could see that he knew everyone.
Minna could see that he would like to know everyone, but
Lars doesn't traffic in favors.

Favors are for politicians, he says.

Minna says, *But it's just a rehearsal space.*

Lars says, *One day it's rehearsal space, the next . . .*

The conversation goes on like that.

Minna pesters.

Lars relents, but only a little.

Lars says that he can call up Tim.

Minna waits by the phone.

Minna changes an A string.

Minna drinks her coffee.

The phone doesn't ring.

Minna goes for a walk.

The phone doesn't ring.

The phone is dead.

Minna checks the SIM card.

The SIM card's working.

Amager Strandpark is shrouded in sea fog.

Amager Strandpark is full of architect-designed bunkers.

Amager Strandpark wants to look like Husby Dunes.

Husby Dunes used to be part of the Atlantic Wall.

Husby Dunes used to be a war zone.

Amager Strandpark makes itself pretty with a tragic backdrop.

Minna doesn't like Amager Strandpark.

Minna really likes the Sound.

Minna loves the sea, the gulls, the salt.

Minna is a bit of a water person, and now her pocket beeps.

Minna looks at her cellphone.

Lars has sent a text.

Tim's on Bornholm, it says.

Minna was prepared for something like that, but

Minna wasn't prepared for what comes next:
Lars writes, *I think we should stop seeing each other.*
Minna reads it again, but that's what it says.
Lars is breaking up with a text.
Minna cannot breathe.
Minna has to sit down on an artificial dune.
Minna writes, *Now I don't understand.*
Minna calls on the phone.
There's no signal.
Minna waits for an answer.
The cell is dead, and so she sits there:
Amager Strandpark is Husby Dunes meets Omaha Beach.
Amager Strandpark is full of savage dogs trying to
flush something out.
Amager Strandpark is a battlefield of wounded women.

*

Minna has gotten Lars to elaborate on his text.
Lars has written, *But I'm not really in love with you.*
Lars has always understood how to cut to the chase.
Minna can't wring any more out of him.
Lars is a wall.
Lars is a porcupine.
Minna lies in bed.
The bed's the only place she wants to lie.
Minna hates that he began the sentence with *But*.
Minna feels that there was a lot missing before *But*, but
Minna should have apparently known better.
Men are also lucky that they possess the sperm.
Men can go far with the sperm.

Men with full sacks play hard to get.
Men with full sacks turn tail, but
Minna can manage without them.
Minna's a composer.
Minna feels her larynx.
The larynx isn't willing.
Minna can hear her neighbor come home.
Minna places an ear against the wall.
The neighbor dumps his groceries on the table.
The neighbor takes a leak.
Minna puts Bach on the stereo.
Minna turns up Bach.
The neighbor is there instantly.
Bach's cello suites are playing.
Minna's fingers are deep in the wound.
Minna looks at the portrait of Lars.
The portrait's from the paper.
Lars is good at growing a beard.
Lars sits there with his beard.
Lars's mouth is a soft wet brushstroke.
Chest hair forces his T-shirt upward.
The beard wanders downward away from his chin.
An Adam's apple lies in the middle of the hair.
Minna's had it in her mouth.
Minna's tasted it.
Minna's submitted, but
Lars looks out at someone who's not her.
Lars regards his reader.
It's not her.
Minna's tormenting herself.

Minna feels that Lars is a hit-and-run driver.
The hit-and-run driver has suffered at most a dented fender.
Minna savors her injuries.
Her heart is spot bleeding.
Her mouth stands agape.
Minna comforts herself.
Minna has the music, after all.
No one can take the music from her.
The music's an existential lifeline.
Minna would just rather have a child.
Minna ought to be glad for what she's got.
Minna would just rather have a child.
Once upon a time, composers were sufficient unto themselves.
Composers didn't need to have children.
The tendency has changed:
Minna should take it upon herself to have a child.
Minna looks at the bookcase.
Minna grabs the first book under B.
Ingmar Bergman opens up for her.
Bergman's wearing the beret.
Bergman's gaze peers deep into Minna.
Bergman wants to get in under Minna's persona.
Minna's persona attempts to make way for him.
Minna wants Bergman all the way inside.
Bach plays.
The neighbor thumps.
Bergman drills.
Minna keeps all superfluous organs to the side.
Bergman says, *I drill, but . . .*
The drill breaks, or else I don't dare drill deep enough.

Minna's managed the impossible:
Bergman can't find the woman in Minna.
The mother won't turn up.
The mother, the whore, the witch.
Minna lifts up her blouse a little.
Bergman shakes his head.
Minna stuffs him up under the blouse.
Bergman doesn't protest.
Bergman makes himself comfortable.
Bergman whispers sweet words to her.
Bergman's words don't work.
Minna's lower lip quivers.
Minna whispers, *I used to sing.*

*

Minna hasn't been out of her flat in three days.
Minna's sent a lot of texts.
Minna's asked Lars to tell her what was supposed to be in front of *But*.
Lars doesn't reply.
Lars won't budge an inch.
Lars was otherwise so mellow.
Minna recalls when they last saw each other.
Minna and Lars lay in bed.
Minna stroked his beard.
Minna read and interpreted.
Lars just needs time.
Minna decides to send Lars an email.
Minna writes, *I think we should meet and talk about it.*
Minna writes, *We can always of course be friends.*

Minna writes, *I miss you so*.
It's wrong to write that, yet she's written it regardless.
It thunders through the ether.
The email's directional.
Minna's ashamed.
The rehearsal space is gone.
Tim's on Bornholm.
Minna's got no money.
Minna's got no boyfriend.
Minna's got only herself, and now she's going out.
Minna goes down the stairs.
Minna goes down to her bike.
The bike stands in the backyard.
The backyard amplifies all sound.
The neighbors' orgasms, the magpies, the pigeons dominate.
Minna puts on her bike helmet.
Minna bikes onto Amagerbrogade.
Minna walks through the revolving doors into the
Royal Library.
Minna wants to concentrate.
The young female students are wearing high heels.
The heels bang against the floor.
Minna despises the students' high heels.
Minna despises their catwalk character.
Minna doesn't think they've studied what they ought to.
Minna fiddles with her sonata.
Minna picks long hairs from her blouse.
Minna waits for news from Lars.
Karin's sent her an email.
Karin sends lots of emails every day.

Karin's emails are long.
Karin tells about her life in the country.
Minna's with her in the bedroom.
Minna's with her at handball in the gym.
Minna isn't shielded from anything.
Karin uses Minna as a diary.
Karin's everyday life will take over Minna's.
Minna makes a rare quick decision.
Minna writes, *Dear Karin.*
It's not you.
It's me.
Minna breaks up with Karin.
All things must have an end.
A worm has two.
Minna doesn't write that last bit.
One shouldn't hurt others unnecessarily.
One should above all be kind.
Minna would rather not be anything but.
Minna's hardly anything but.
The email thunders through the ether toward Karin.
That's as it should be, thinks Minna.
The ether is full of malicious messages.
The ether hums with break-ups and loss.
The ether is knives being thrown.
The ether is blood surging back.
Minna has wounded a creature.
Minna stares out on the canal.
Minna listens to the banging heels.
Minna needs to go to the bathroom.

*

Minna's peed.
Minna's back in her place.
Minna sits and feels the pain.
The pain's a contagion.
The borders recede.
Cynicism buds.
Pointlessness grimaces!
Minna's snuck Bergman out of her bag.
Minna's got to concentrate.
Someone waves from behind the panoramic glass.
Jette's standing with a bakery bag.
Coffee's to be drunk on the quay.
Jette's a classically trained harpist.
Jette's given up finding rehearsal space.
The harp's stood in the way her entire life.
Minna knows the feeling.
Minna's had the same experience with grand pianos, but
Grand pianos grow on trees.
Harps are exclusive.
Harps are for fairies, angels, and the frigid.
Jette's erotic.
Jette calls her boyfriends *lovers*.
Jette's boyfriends are married to other women.
Jette's studying composition in Reading Room North.
Minna writes paper sonatas in Reading Room East.
Minna and Jette drink coffee together.
The relationship isn't supposed to get serious.
Jette talks too much about bodies.
Jette has an IUD in her genital tract.
Jette has discharges and domestic obligations.

Jette needs a weekend escape with a lover.
Jette fears vaginal dryness.
The uterus is an abandoned studio flat.
The vagina's the gateway to the enjoyment of all things.
Jette says, *Don't you agree?*
Minna says, *Isn't that a balloon?*
Minna points to a spot above the harbor.
Jette's content with the two kids she has.
Enough's enough, says Jette.
Jette has two kids, thinks Minna.
Minna has a hard time getting up from the quay.
Minna feels like a horse.
Minna says, *I think it was Bugs Bunny.*
Jette goes through the door into the Royal Library.
Minna stands there like a fly in the ointment, and then she has to pee.
Minna has to really pee, and it has to happen fast.

*

Minna has to go to the john twice a day on average when she works at the Royal Library.
Minna pees.
Minna fills her water bottle from the tap.
Minna leaves the john.
Minna's surrounded by a couple hundred police officers in mufti.
The officers are with the Danish National Police.
The officers stand at attention in the buffet area.
The officers are at a conference in the Karen Blixen Meeting Room.
Minna watches the deputy commissioner eat a fish roll.
Minna slopes through the crowd.

Minna's a relic.
Minna spools up across two hundred officers.
Minna towers over four hundred sperm-filled sacs.
The officers' laughter bursts through the room.
Jens Peter Jacobsen shudders.
Hans Christian Andersen ditto.
Yard upon yard of shelving turns its back.
Minna writes tonal rows.
Minna sweats.
Minna works like a horse.
Minna heaves the tones around on the paper.
Minna clears her throat.
Minna clears her throat a little more.
The girl to her left shushes her.
Minna packs up and rides downstairs.
Minna enters the revolving doors from one side.
A police officer enters from the other.
Minna revolves around with the officer.
Minna is walking and going round.
The revolving door mechanism feels defective.
The officer gets his foot caught.
The revolving door stops heavily.
The revolving door spits Minna out like a clay pigeon.
Iceland Wharf lies far beneath Minna.
Iceland Wharf shines flat and practical.
Minna sees far beneath her the mermaid on the quay.
Minna looks out across the city.
Minna floats.
Minna's in flight over Copenhagen.
Minna's an instance of female buoyancy and helium.

*

Lars is as silent as the grave, but
Karin's answered quickly.
Minna's seated herself in her kitchen at home.
Minna doesn't dare open the email from Karin.
Karin plays accordion.
Minna and Karin took a class together.
Karin latched on to Minna.
Minna is somewhat of a host species.
Minna has now finally told Karin to stop.
The decision's good enough.
The decision was just made too late.
Karin feels bad now.
Karin's self-worth has been damaged.
Karin's self-worth is Jutlandic.
Karin brags about motocross, sex, and pork sausage.
Karin's married to a farmer.
The farmer's bought up the parish.
The parish belongs to Karin.
Karin drinks tall boys.
Karin plays folk dances.
Karin's on the gym board.
Karin sticks her hand all the way up her neighbor.
Karin grasps the inner udder.
Karin milks.
Karin pinches and squeezes.
The teat yields.
The teat's tugged long and white.
The teat grows tender and stiff.
The teat grows so tired in the end.

Minna also wrote her, *Now relax*, but
Karin doesn't need to restrain herself:
Karin goes to zumba.
Minna was right to break up with her.
A person ought to defend herself.
Minna opens the email from Karin.
Minna's right.
Karin writes nasty things about Minna.
Minna can't for instance land a man.
Men don't want women like Minna.
Age will drag you down!!! Karin writes.
Barrenness will haunt you!!! Karin writes, and continues:
Minna doesn't know how to live.
Minna only knows how to think.
Karin's got everything that Minna wants.
Karin's got a dog, a man, and kids.
Karin's got 500 acres of land.
Minna's got zilch.
Minna's lonely, a failure, and deserves to be pissed on.
Karin pisses.
Minna thinks that should suffice.
People are getting worse and worse.
Middle fingers poke out of car windows.
Small dogs shit before her entryway.
Young men shout *whore*.
The three Billy Goats Gruff play havoc in nice folks' sunrooms.
People's faces look kind.
People's faces *aren't* kind.
Minna wants to reply.
Minna wants to write nasty things too, but

Minna thinks enough's enough.
Minna longs for shut traps.
Minna longs for stillness and beauty.
Minna seats herself by the window.
Minna looks down on the street.
Minna watches a tiny dog back up to the curbstone and gently squeeze out a turd.

*

Night has descended on Amager.
Denmark is laid in darkness.
The Sound flows softly.
The planes take off and land.
Minna awakens.
Minna gasps.
Lars was in the dream.
Minna and Lars were at the beach.
Minna was buried with just her head free.
The sea was rough at the foot of the dune.
The sea raged, foaming white.
Dad stood in the breakers and waved.
Minna wanted to grab Lars in her haste.
Minna wriggled her arms.
The arms wouldn't budge.
Lars pelted her with sand.
Lars patted her hard with a shovel.
Lars poured water over her.
Lars used her to build a sandcastle.
The wave reached land.
The wave reached land and trickled slowly.

The beads of gravel rattled.
Dad vanished.
Minna awoke.
Minna turned on the light, and now it is quiet.
Amager steams with rain.
The rain refracts off the manholes.
Minna never bakes cake.
Minna gets up to bake a cake.
Minna bakes a cake in the middle of the night.
Cake is the opiate of the people.

*

Jette sits on the quay and is intimate.
Minna's brought cake for coffee.
Minna unwraps the tinfoil from a piece of cake.
The tinfoil feels childish.
The cake isn't very good either.
Jette's been to a seminar.
Jette has a new lover.
The lover's Russian.
The Russian's as hot as fresh borscht.
The Russian's French is good.
Jette's got Reds in her pleasure pavilion, thinks Minna.
Minna looks at the mermaid on the quay.
The mermaid is green.
The mermaid cannot swim.
The mermaid would sink to the bottom immediately.
Minna says, *Such sun!*
Jette says, *What about you?*
Minna says, *I'm working on the paper sonata.*

Minna knows perfectly well that Jette means sex.
Minna knows perfectly well that Jette wants to trade moisture.
Minna knows perfectly well that Jette's leading on points.
Karin too.
Minna understands completely.
It's something to do with physics.
It's something to do as well with the soul.
Minna can't explain it.
Minna bloody won't explain it either.
Minna looks at the mermaid.
The mermaid's tailfin is cast in bronze.
The mermaid's tailfin can't slap.
The world is a suit of clothes.
The clothes too tight.
The corneas drying out.
Minna stretches: *Work calls.*
Jette says, *Leaving already?*
Minna is.
Minna disappears up to the reading room.
Minna stares at her inbox.
Everyone writes and no one answers, thinks Minna.
Elisabeth's written.
Elisabeth will treat her to a cup of tea.
Elisabeth is Minna's big sister.
Karin, Elisabeth, and Jette, thinks Minna.
Women in their prime.
Women with the right to vote.
Women with educations.
Women with their own needs.
Women with herb gardens and the pill.

Steamrollers, thinks Minna.
One mustn't think like that.
Women are awful to women, Minna's mother's always said.
Mom's right, but
Women are tough to swallow.
Minna doesn't understand why men like women.
Women want to cross the finish line first.
Women want to look good on the podium.
Women are in the running, but
Minna's otherworldly.
Minna's a composer.
Minna's not a mother.
Minna doesn't have a mothers' group.
Minna sees the mothers' group often.
The mothers' group takes walks in Amager.
The mothers' group drives in formation.
The mothers' group is scared of getting fat.
The mothers' group goes jogging with their baby buggies.
The mothers' group eats cake at the café.
The mothers' group contends gently for the view.
The baby buggies pad the façade.
The baby buggies form a breastwork.
Minna fears the mothers' group.
Minna cannot say that out loud.
Minna doesn't have a child.
Minna can't let herself say anything.
Minna's not home free.
Minna once won a prize for some chamber music.
Minna would rather have gotten a license to live.

*

Minna's laid herself down on the couch.
Minna looks forward:
The prospect's hazy.
Minna looks backward:
Time has passed.
Minna recalls the Bay of Aarhus.
Minna recalls Dad:
Dad and Minna hike through Marselisborg Forest.
Dad and Minna hike down to Ballehage Beach.
Dad and Minna sniff the anemones.
Dad and Minna change into their bathing suits.
Dad and Minna position themselves on the pier.
Dad and Minna inhale the salt.
The wind's taken hold of Dad's hair.
The wind whips round Minna's ditto.
Dad and Minna stand with arms extended.
Dad's armpits hairy.
Minna's bathing suit with balloon effect.
Dad's finger toward the horizon: *Helgenæs!*
Minna takes a running jump.
Minna shoots out into the bay.
Dad's a water bomb.
Dad and Minna dive.
Dad and Minna splash each other.
Dad and Minna can do anything, but
Minna grew up.
Minna had to bathe alone.
Minna hiked through Marselisborg Forest.
Minna wanted to hike down to Ballehage, but
Minna met a roe deer.

The deer stood on a bluff.
The deer stood stock-still and stared at Minna.
Minna stood stock-still and stared at the deer.
The deer was a creature of the deep forest.
The deer was mild and moist of gaze.
Minna was mild and moist of gaze.
The deer's legs like stalks.
The deer's fur in the sun.
Minna's hair in the wind.
The forest was empty when the deer departed.
Minna looked across the bay.
Minna inhaled the salt.
Minna gazed at the pier.
Minna picked mushrooms from half-rotted stumps.
Minna threw her arms around a beech tree.
Love ought to find its voice again.
Loss ought to fade out, but
Loss and love are connected, Minna thinks.
Minna lies in Amager.
Minna turns on her side.
Love presupposes loss.
Minna deeply misses Lars.
The pain's connected to hope.
Hope is light green.
Hope's a roe deer on a bluff.
Someone has got to love, thinks Minna.
Someone's got to fight.

*

Minna's got a lot to fight.
Lars has deleted her.
Minna's no longer friends with Lars.
Lars has spoken.
Minna's been expunged.
Lars has disappeared from her wall, but
Minna can see Lars everywhere.
Lars hangs out with the others.
Lars invites people for beer.
That's awful enough.
This is worse:
Lars comments on everything Linda Lund says.
Linda Lund also attended the conservatory.
Minna was good at piano.
Linda was good at guitar, but
Linda's better suited to the music industry.
Minna can screw a reporter and still not get her picture in the paper.
Linda Lund's just got to cross the street.
Linda's sex appeal is undeniable.
Minna can feel Linda's sex in everything.
Sex is power.
Sex is currency.
Linda is loaded.
The world's a stage.
The stage is Linda's.
No one may block the view of Linda.
Minna knows that.
Minna and Linda run into each other now and then.
Minna's still got scars from the last time.

Minna stood there with her score.
Minna was making for the stage.
Minna was supposed to perform just like the others, but
Minna ran into Linda in the wings.
Linda pulled out a mental machete.
Linda slashed a couple times.
Linda said, *That dress will blend into the curtain.*
Linda said, *What's your name again?*
Minna almost couldn't perform afterward.
Lars is in a fix.
Lars congratulates Linda on her birthday.
Linda replies, *Thanks for last night, kiss kiss.*
Lars writes, *Nice!*
Linda says, *It certainly was.*
Lars says, *Rock on, babe!*
Linda's a cannonball in jacket and skirt.
Lars is a hypnotized reporter.
Minna sits and gasps.
Karin sits on the grill of her 4 x 4.
Karin sits and smiles on her 4 x 4.
Minna unfriends vehicle and Karin both.
Minna unfriends Linda Lund too.
Minna doesn't want to be an unwilling witness!
Minna doesn't want her nose rubbed in the piss.
Minna unfriends another two people.
Minna unfriends more.
Minna unfriends Britta.
Britta's an old schoolmate.
Britta's written,
Britta's put the pork loin on the Weber.

Minna can no longer leave well enough alone, but
The unfriendings provide no relief.
Minna's been unfriended herself.
The pain of unfriending's unbearable.
Minna misses Lars.
Lars has inflicted a trauma.
Minna's in love with someone who's traumatized her.
Minna reckons that makes her a masochist.
Minna doesn't want to be a masochist.
Minna wants to be a human being, but
Minna's expunged.
It hurts so much, Minna whispers.
Minna goes into the shower.
Minna lets the water run, and then she stands there:
Minna with her lips turned toward the tiles.
Minna with blood on her hands.
Minna with soap in her eyes.
Minna with no roe deer.

*

The ringmaster of a flea circus lets the artists suck his blood.
Bergman strokes Minna on the cheek.
A daydreamer isn't an artist except in his dreams.
Bergman reaches for the buttermilk.
Bergman has indigestion.
Minna has a burnt taste in her mouth.
Bergman whispers, *I contain too much humanity.*
The days are long, large, light.
They're as substantial as cows, as some sort of bloody big animal.
Minna snuggles up to Bergman.

Dad strokes Minna's cheek.
Dad settles himself on his rock.
Dad understands.
Dad isn't scared.

*

Minna's read Bergman for a couple days.
Minna's tired of lying in bed.
Minna checks her email.
Minna's gotten lots of email.
Mom and Jette have written.
Elisabeth's written, and look here:
Karin's written.
That was expected.
Minna doesn't know if she'll read Karin's missive.
The street clatters with bikes and cars.
The sun's risen over Amager Strandpark.
Baresso's opened.
The coffees to go are warming palms.
The coffees to go are out walking.
The cellphones, the blankies, the coffees to go.
People trickle toward City Hall Square.
People look like shoals of shiny herring.
People press on with sand and sleep in their eyes.
Minna eats a cracker.
Karin's missive awaits.
Karin wants to be nasty.
Karin wants to upset her applecart, but
Minna's cart has no apples.
The damage has been done.

Lars has disappeared.
Linda's getting laid.
Karin's got a dog.
Karin takes walks with her dog on the beach.
The dog'll fetch a stick for Karin.
The dog whips back and forth.
Karin throws farther and farther.
The dog doesn't hold back.
Karin casts the stick into the ocean.
The dog throws itself in.
Karin keeps casting the stick.
The dog keeps bounding.
It could continue this way forever, but
Minna's got to get to it.
Minna reads:
Karin's discovered that she's been unfriended.
Karin's hurt.
Karin repeats the gist from last time.
Karin just spices the gist up a bit:
Jutland women can fuck!!!
Music should be popular!!!
Music shouldn't be deep!!!
KARIN LOVES BRYAN ADAMS!!!
Minna swallows her cracker.
Karin keeps going: *I feel bad for you!!!*
Karin can say more: *You'll come to regret it!!!*
Minna's counted Karin's exclamation points.
The email contains fifty-six exclamation points.
That's plenty, but
Minna doesn't even feel like crying.

Minna's anesthetized to blows.
Minna looks out the window.
Minna looks down upon the transport tsunami.
The network people whizz away.
The network people have got business cards.
A chink suffices.
The darkness yields willingly, but
Network hearts don't have the time.
Minna considers her hands.
Minna thinks her hands resemble thimbles.
Minna's hands *are* thimbles.
Thimbles can't grab.
The world around is laid with tile.
Network people are highly polished.
Minna shakes herself.
Minna tests her grasping power on her hair.
Her fingers can still grab herself hard.
Better than nothing, thinks Minna, and sits down.

*

Paper sonatas don't write themselves.
Minna bikes to the Royal Library.
The city's blazing hot from the sun.
The cell's blazing hot from messages.
Elisabeth's after her.
Elisabeth's ten years older than Minna.
Elisabeth's married to a successful optician.
Elisabeth lives in the Potato Row Houses.
The optician's skinny and dry.
Minna understands him.

The optician's a guest in his own home.
Guests have it rough at Elisabeth's.
Shoes have to be taken off in the hallway.
Shoes must never cross the threshold.
The guest has to pee.
The guest really has to pee.
The john lies on the far side of the utility room.
The shoes have to be removed anyway.
The shoes have to be put on and taken off without leaning
on the walls.
The walls in the hallway must not get grime spots.
The bench in the hallway must not have any bottoms upon it.
The bench is *not* to sit on.
The bench is there to create harmony in the hallway.
The guest is barefoot and entering a house full of rules.
Elisabeth makes the rules.
No one else has permission to make rules in the house.
Cutlery must not clink against the service.
The table must not be wiped with a wet rag.
Books must be bound in dust jackets.
Fingers must not touch the pictures.
The coffee mugs must not stand without coasters underneath.
The coffee mugs must not contain coffee.
Coffee is forbidden at Elisabeth's.
Everyone must drink tea.
The optician gets the trots from tea, but
The optician must remove his shoes before he runs to the john.
The optician struggles with his suede shoes in the hallway.
The optician's afraid to place his fingers anywhere.
The optician just reaches the toilet in his stocking feet.

The shit runs out of him like green tea.
Elisabeth shouts, *Is that you, honey?*
The shit runs and runs.
The optician considers whether he dares to shit any more.
Elisabeth shouts, *Is that you who came home, honey?*
The optician reaches for the toilet paper.
The optician remembers to tear it off in a straight line.
The optician's lonesome, completely without allies.
Elisabeth and the optician have neither dog nor kids.
It's sad, but
One thing is certain:
Kids set their bottoms everywhere.
Elisabeth's turning fifty besides.
Elisabeth's still pretty.
Elisabeth's hair is fair like Minna's, but
Elisabeth's hair doesn't dare curl.
Elisabeth is illuminated.
Elisabeth is an act of will.
Elisabeth's sent Minna a stream of messages.
Minna sits on her bike and reads them.
Minna approaches Knippel Bridge.
Minna has one hand on the handlebars.
Minna has one eye on the display.
Elisabeth wants her to phone.
Elisabeth wants her to drop by.
Minna passes the Stock Exchange.
Minna holds for a bus.
Minna MUST ring between two and four.
Minna MUST NOT ring at any other time.
Elisabeth practices yoga and meditates.

The day is scheduled.
Elisabeth says it's all about respecting others' needs.
Minna understands:
Lars has a need to screw a celebrity.
Jette has a need to share her sex life.
Karin has a need to take up space out in the country.
Linda Lund has a need for an audience.
Minna has to get up to stand on the pedals.
Minna is honked at.
Minna bikes out into the intersection by the Stock Exchange.
Elisabeth pursues her.
Elisabeth was an only child for ten years.
Elisabeth's still an only child.
Elisabeth isn't healthier than Karin.
Karin requires a host animal.
Elisabeth requires weak creatures.
Weak creatures can defer their needs.
Elisabeth has to be done with hers first.
Elisabeth will never be done with hers.
Elisabeth was never at Ballehage Beach either.
The sand was a mess, but
Dad and Minna could dive.
Minna's not weak.
Minna won't!
The traffic roars around Minna.
The traffic's unsafe.
Minna turns past Det Røde Palæ.
Minna bikes and taps.
Minna taps, *I'm just on my bike.*
Elisabeth orders her to call anyway.

Minna turns off her cell.
Minna drops the cell into her bag.
The bag trembles in the bike basket.
Minna trembles on the bike, but
Paper sonatas don't write themselves.

*

The quay oozes female students.
The police officers are back in Karen Blixen.
The officers stand smoking on the quay.
The officers keep an eagle eye on the students.
The students don't see the officers.
The students cast their hair about.
Their hair flips from side to side.
The students get to their feet.
The officers get to their feet.
The students' legs grow long.
The officers' pants have pockets.
The officers tug at their pockets.
The officers camouflage their sperm-filled bits.
Minna and Jette sit *sans camouflage* in the midst of it all.
Jette's eyes are insistent.
Minna has a hard time relaxing.
The legs biking.
The arms warding off blows.
The body full of vim.
The soul supposed to sit still.
It ain't easy.
Jette notices that sort of thing.
Jette says, *You seem stressed out*.

Minna replies, *I've got a little too much going on.*
Jette says, *Tell, tell!*
Minna says, *Oh, you know . . .*
Jette says, *You shouldn't walk around keeping everything bottled up.*
Minna says, *The paper sonata's bumping along.*
Minna says that she'll buy a keyboard.
Jette thinks she could just use her Mac.
Macs have a program for composers.
Macs are easy to figure out.
Minna doesn't want to say that she can't figure them out.
Minna doesn't want to satisfy Jette's need to know better.
Minna says, *It's my sister, that's all.*
Minna points at the mermaid on the quay.
The mermaid by the Royal Library is prettier than Langelinie's.
The mermaid by the Royal Library is anything but charming.
The mermaid by the Royal Library can do somersaults.
The mermaid has just come ashore.
The quay is a rock.
The mermaid has a hold, but
The world makes it tough.
Anne Marie Carl-Nielsen made the mermaid.
Anne Marie Carl-Nielsen was kind to animals.
Anne Marie Carl-Nielsen was married to Carl Nielsen.
Anne Marie Carl-Nielsen was a great sculptor.
Carl Nielsen was a great composer.
Carl Nielsen wasn't an easy man to be married to, says Minna.
Carl Nielsen couldn't ignore his needs.
Carl was a firecracker.
Carl was a billy goat.

Anne Marie sculpted horses in Jutland.
Carl had ladies visit in Copenhagen.
Anne Marie's horses got bigger and bigger.
Carl's ladies got rifer and rifer.
Anne Marie placed herself beneath the horses.
Carl placed himself beneath the ladies.
Anne Marie had to learn to forgive.
Anne Marie had to stomach it.
The mermaid casts herself up out of the sea.
The mermaid contracts like a muscle before it explodes.
The mermaid clings to dry land, angry and insecure.
The mermaid is pure wet will.
She gasps.
She stares at the quay's young people.
Carl Nielsen was a handsome man, says Jette.
Carl Nielsen was stumpy, says Minna.
Carl Nielsen could've been my lover, says Jette.
The conversation's taken a familiar turn.
The Russian has a wife in Moscow.
The wife in Moscow doesn't know a thing.
Minna looks at the mermaid.
The mermaid knows all.

*

Minna's mother lives in Aarhus.
Minna's from Jutland, just like Karin.
Minna's just not from Jutland in the same way.
Minna's from Marselisborg Forest.
Minna's an old man's daughter.
Minna's a younger widow's caboose.

Mom's still a widow, but
Mom's got a boyfriend.
The boyfriend's name is Finn.
Finn and Mom go to museums.
Finn and Mom attend folk high school.
Finn and Mom each live alone.
Mom's too old for the whole package.
Finn would otherwise be interested, but
Mom's master in her own home.
Mom's also good at staying in touch.
Mom's taken a computer class at the Senior Club.
Mom's on Facebook.
Mom's got a blog.
Mom can text.
Elisabeth says you're feeling poorly, she writes.
Elisabeth's worried, she writes.
Mom's worried too.
Minna stands in the hallway and reads.
Minna considers getting a cat.
The cat'd come stealing in from the living room.
The cat'd rub up against Minna's leg.
The cat and Bergman, Minna thinks.
Minna collapses on the couch.
Bergman rests on the table.
Bergman's there for the grasping.
You'll do what's needed, he says.
Failures can have a fresh, bitter taste, he says.
Minna lays him to her breast.
Bergman makes himself at home there.
Minna closes her eyes:

Minna can hear the cars down on the street.
Minna can hear herself drawing breath.
Bergman curls up into a ball.
Minna dozes off.
Minna dreams of a house on a hill.
The yard bulges with fruit and lilacs.
Phlox, mallow, iris blossoming.
The gable wall glows with English roses.
The fjord flashes at the foot of the hill.
Minna's seated on the patio.
The boats tack into the wind.
The henhouse has been whitewashed.
The henhouse is the rehearsal space.
The grand piano stands plumb in the middle.
Minna turns her face toward the sun.
Minna's chest arches over her heart.
The heart is lovely in its dissolution.
The heart has weathered the storm.
Minna listens to the interior of the house.
The door's opened and shut.
Keys are laid upon the table.
Someone's approaching the patio door.
Lars stands there smiling.
Lars bends over his woman.
Lars caresses his woman's belly.
The baby kicks inside.
The reaper-binder rattles outside.
The skylarks sing high in the air.
The rifle club's meeting in the gravel pit.
The rifle club shoots clay pigeons.

The clay pigeons whizz across the landscape.
The clay pigeons are shot or shatter when they fall.
The clay pigeons fall and fall.
Minna's wakened by a muffled thud on the floor.
It's Bergman.
It's Monday, Minna remembers.
She's in Amager, she remembers.

*

It's a miracle.
Elisabeth's visiting Minna's flat.
Elisabeth stands in the middle of the living room.
Elisabeth's in stocking feet.
The face as hard as enamel.
Elisabeth's rage is a legend in the family.
The examples are legion:
Elisabeth removes bikes in Potato Row.
Nothing may shade the house.
Nothing may destroy the harmony of the façade.
Elisabeth doesn't move the bikes a couple yards.
Elisabeth walks around to other streets with the bikes.
No one should think they're safe.
Elisabeth threatens people with lawsuits and psychotic episodes.
Elisabeth drives people to numerologists, and even worse:
Elisabeth once made Mom have a breakdown over a piece of royal porcelain.
Elisabeth's aligned the stars on her side, and now she stands in the living room:
Dust rises: *Didn't I tell you to call?*
Elisabeth continues, *Didn't I tell you to come by?*

Minna proffers tea.
Elisabeth sets her purse down on the coffee table.
Elisabeth's eyes flit from the dirty laundry to Bach.
Elisabeth's eyes need to shut for a bit.
Minna edges past her sister.
Minna pours calcified water into two mugs from IKEA.
Minna stuffs in the teabags.
Minna walks back to the living room.
Elisabeth has seated herself.
Minna sets a mug before her.
Elisabeth doesn't want the tea.
The tea ought to be green, *And why didn't you call me then?*
Minna doesn't manage to answer.
Elisabeth cranks up the language.
The language lashes Minna.
The language is a castigation.
Minna sips her tea.
Sisters should be there for each other, Elisabeth says.
Sisters should save each other from the muck.
Minna's life gleams with muck, *Is it that reporter?*
Minna says that that might be it.
Elisabeth sighs.
Elisabeth reaches for her purse.
Minna knows what's coming: the prescription.
Elisabeth's into Ayurvedic medicine.
Ayurvedic medicine stems from India.
Ayurvedic medicine divides people into types.
Elisabeth is fire, Elisabeth says.
Minna's mud.
No one's surprised.

Elisabeth's been to the Bookstore of the Unknown.
Elisabeth's bought a book about demons.
The demons are Indian.
The book's dust jacket is black.
Elisabeth says that the book will provide Minna with fire.
Indian demons are good at rage.
Demons transform through destruction.
Minna watches her sister's face: it actually opens up.
The face is a soup pot of crazy ideas.
The sister feels certain the reporter can be exorcized.
Minna will see, it'll be a relief.
Minna looks at the book and understands.
Minna's a weak creature.
Elisabeth's stronger.
Minna thanks her.
Minna's a pleaser.
Elisabeth's rage is a legend in the family, but
Elisabeth's doing better now.
Elisabeth gets up and adjusts her clothing.
A vacuum cleaner wouldn't hurt, Elisabeth says.
Minna nods.
Aarhus is still on the map, Elisabeth says.
Minna nods.
Dad got to be old as the hills.
Minna nods.
Life goes on.
Minna nods.
It's really late, her sister says.
Minna nods and nods and nods.

*

Elisabeth's demons lie on the night table.
Minna can't sleep.
The demons sneak about in the dark.
The demons reek of soot.
Minna switches on the light and opens the door to the
kitchen stairs.
Minna goes down into the backyard and its twilight.
The man in number eight's watching soccer.
The woman in number four's having sex.
The stars twinkle.
The trashcan gapes.
Minna casts the demons from her and closes the lid.
Minna opens the lid again.
Minna jams the book under a bag.
It's not enough.
Minna jams it farther down.
Minna can feel the trash around her hand.
Minna feels the trash's soft and hard parts.
Minna gets damp fingers.
Minna gets her upper arm in.
Minna thinks of vets and midwives.
Minna's as deep down as she can get.
Minna releases the book.
The book's wedged in there deep down.
Minna hauls up her damp arm.
Minna averts her face from the stench.
Minna presses the lid down hard.
The man in number eight scores.
The woman in number four ditto.
Minna goes back upstairs.

Minna scrubs herself.
Minna goes to bed.
Minna can't sleep.
You never know with demons.
Demons are parasites.
Parasites need individuals.
Minna knows that.
Minna's an individual herself.
Minna's one individual among millions.
Minna's a gnu on the savannah.
Minna's a herring in a barrel, but even worse:
Minna places her hands across her eyes.
Minna feels something: *Was that hair?*
Minna slips out to the mirror.
Minna places her face against it, and there she is:
Minna with fur on her face.
Minna in a wild stampede.
Minna on her way over the cliff edge.
The sea waiting below.
Death by drowning.
Her paws paddling and paddling.
The paws cannot, they cannot.
The orchestra plays a psalm.
Minna can no longer sing.
Minna sinks quietly toward the bottom.
Minna doesn't struggle at all.
Minna doesn't understand it herself.
Minna tells her mirror image, *Swim then, God damn it*, but Minna doesn't swim.

*

The sun's shining.
Jette's placed the paper across her knee.
The paper's opened to the culture section.
The front page of the culture section is full of a woman.
The woman is Linda Lund.
Minna balances two cups of coffee.
Jette's busy smoothing out the paper.
Minna's having a hard time getting her legs to bend.
Minna glances at the mermaid's gaping gaze.
Minna glances at Linda.
Linda fills most of the front page.
Linda's shot with an out-of-focus lens.
Linda's mouth is slightly open.
Linda's eyes are deep and alert.
Linda sits and strokes her guitar.
The guitar no longer plays Segovia.
The guitar plays wistful pop.
People love wistful pop.
The guitar's positioned between Linda's legs.
People love Linda's legs.
Minna has goblins in her diaphragm.
Minna turns green.
Minna's terrible to photograph.
Minna's better in person, but
Linda looks lovely in the paper.
Minna can't breathe.
Minna's throat stings.
Jette rustles the paper excessively.
Jette lifts it up.
The paper's right in Minna's face.

Minna sees what Jette wants to show her:
Lars has written the article.
Lars has made the article fill seven columns.
Lars has used the word *sensual* in the headline.
Minna looks toward Christianshavn.
Jette knocks back her coffee.
Things are going well for Linda, Jette says.
Minna's tongue feels cold as bronze.
Minna's body starts shutting down.
The face chilly.
The heart pounding.
The larynx a clenched fist.
Nothing comes out.
Jette asks, *How's Lars, really?*
Minna's fingers tighten around her coffee.
Jette asks, *Do you still see each other?*
Minna has sat down but can't remain sitting.
Minna gets up and hops around a bit.
Minna has to pee.
Minna has to go to the john twice a day on average when she's at the Royal Library.

*

Minna wants to tell someone about her broken heart.
Minna feels pain in the solar plexus of her soul.
Minna needs a hot-water bottle.
Finn answers the phone.
Finn wants to chat.
Finn's a birdwatcher.
Finn's seen a bittern.

Finn knows where the nightingale lives.
Minna asks for Mom.
Mom comes to the phone.
Mom's glad to hear from her.
Minna's just about to cry, but
Mom and Finn have been to the Skaw.
Mom and Finn saw someone famous in a car.
Mom and Finn took a hike on Grenen.
The wind was blowing sand.
The sand got into everything.
Mom says that she misses Minna.
Mom feels like it's been a long time.
The clump in Minna's throat gets bigger.
The clump's a doorstop.
Minna can't say anything.
Mom goes quiet on the other end.
Mom and Minna are quiet together.
Minna whispers that she'll definitely come visit.
It won't be long, Minna says.
Mom says that of course they could come to Copenhagen.
Time's one thing they've got plenty of.
Minna doesn't like that Mom says *they.*
Minna says they'd be very welcome.
Minna says we should go to Copenhagen, Mom says.
Finn's indistinct in the background.
Mom laughs.
Mom tells her about the geraniums.
The geraniums are thriving in the east-facing windows.
The geraniums have an acrid scent in the sun.
The geraniums get photographed.

The geraniums get posted on the web.
Minna should go in and see.
Minna promises to look at Mom's blog.
Minna keeps her promise.
Mom's blog is kept rose pink.
Mom's blog is mostly photos, but
Text sneaks its way in between the geraniums.
Mom's written about her daughters on the blog.
The daughters live far away in Copenhagen.
The elder one's married to an optician.
The younger is unwed.
Mom isn't a grandma.
You can't get everything you wish for, Mom writes.
Minna stares at the text.
The text is more intimate than Mom's Christmas letter to the family.
The text is more naked than Minna's seen Mom in real life.
Nobody really reads it anyhow, Mom must've thought.
Somebody might read it by accident, Mom must've thought.
Both thoughts had appealed.
It started small.
It began as a lift of the skirt.
It took root gradually.
The web's become a diary for Mom.
Mom starts to versify.
Mom writes haiku.
Mom lets it all hang out.
The geraniums are pink and demure, but
Mom's stark naked.
Minna hastens to shut it off.

Minna considers calling up the Senior Club.
The Senior Club ought to explain the gravity to seniors.
The web's a jungle.
The jungle's full of monkeys.
Monkeys love the excrement of others.

*

Lars has had Linda on the front page.
Elisabeth's been in the Bookstore of the Unknown.
Jette sits on the quay.
Mom's on the web too often.
Dad's dead.
Lars has fur on his face, but
Lars's fur isn't quite like Minna's.
Minna's fur is a metaphor.
Lars's fur is real.
Minna's studied portraits.
Lars and Dad have a beard in common, but
Lars smelled of Aqua Velva.
Dad of salt.
Minna's looked at the map of Denmark.
Aarhus nestles in Marselisborg Forest.
Amager's on the other end of the country, or
Amager's in the middle of the country, or
Amager's in any case quiet for a brief moment.
The quiet makes room.
The quiet makes a dome over a moment's clarity.
The clarity lays bare a person.
The person is Minna herself.
Minna hasn't seen her own person for a long time.

Minna's person has split ends.
Minna's person has bags.
The person's hand trembles quietly.
The person's mouth hangs open.
Minna can hear a faint hum.
Minna thinks, *I used to sing . . .*
Minna gives herself the once-over.
Minna benefits from the examination.
Time now for a little holiday.
Other people aren't to join the holiday.
Minna hasn't been to Bornholm since she was fourteen.
Bornholm's almost Sweden.
Bornholm's in the opposite direction.
Bornholm's an island.
Bornholm's well suited to mental catharsis.
Lars will be forgotten.
The family'll have to take care of itself.
The family *can* take care of itself.
Minna orders a ticket to Ystad.
Minna wants to develop an ability to sort people out.
Minna wants an asshole filter.
Minna no longer wants to be a host species.
Minna takes Bergman along.
Bergman can ride in the backpack.

*

Minna's sitting on the train to Ystad.
Minna's feeling chipper.
Minna's running away from it all.
Minna's breaking from the pack.

The pack is evil.
Minna doesn't want to be part of them.
Minna's wistful too.
Minna was sure one grew out of it.
Minna thought as a kid, *As soon as I grow up*, but
Grown-ups are kids who have lots to hide.
Dumb kids become dumb grown-ups.
Evil kids = evil grown-ups.
Minna gets the connection.
Minna walks around among ordinary people.
Ordinary people cheat on their taxes.
Ordinary people visit swinger clubs.
Ordinary people flee the scene of the crime.
Ordinary people enlist in the Nordland Regiment of the SS.
Ordinary people are quislings, collaborators, camp followers.
Ordinary people just need a stage.
The pig performs gladly.
Cowards are also in good supply.
Minna doesn't get how she could have looked past it.
Minna's clear-sighted enough.
Minna's watched TV.
Minna followed the war in the Balkans.
Minna watched neighbors outing each other to Serbian militias.
One day you're tending cabbage together in the backyard.
The next you're on a bus headed for a mass grave.
Your best friend's a chameleon.
Evil's a state that can be conjured.
Evil exists.
Minna supposes she's tarred with the same brush.
Karin's not exactly without stain either.

Elisabeth is family.
Lars could've been.
Minna realizes that it's all about sorting.
Minna's got to judge people one at a time.
Minna wants to learn not to trust.
That'll all be over now.
The last narcissist's gotten her to clap.
The last Jutlander's taken up residence in her inbox.
The last nymphomaniac.
The last reporter.
Indian demons.
Billy goats.
Kamikaze pilots.
Thieves in the night:
It's over!
Minna feels her backbone grow.
Minna's backbone sends out roots and shoots.
Minna's backbone blossoms.
Minna looks out upon the southern Swedish landscape.
The landscape drifts past like a fog.
Grown-ups are kids who become like animals, Minna thinks.
Minna tries dozing.
The train's got a school camp on board.
The school camp's blocked all exits.
The teacher screams that the school camp has to settle down a bit.
The teacher screams, *SO SIT DOWN, FREDERIK!*
The teacher screams, *THERE ARE OTHER PEOPLE ON THE TRAIN!*
That might be so, Minna thinks, but
Bergman's the only human on the train.
Bergman lies on her lap.

Dread makes the dreaded real.
That's true – or . . .
Minna listens to the school camp.
Minna dreaded *not* having a kid.
The school camp relieves the fear.
Kids are sweet, but
Kids reflect their parents' seamy side.
Bergman knows that.
Bergman had nine kids.
Bergman had to make films to get away from his kids.
Minna shouldn't be down in the mouth.
Anne Marie Carl-Nielsen's also along on the trip.
Anne Marie's along in Minna's mind.
Anne Marie preferred animals.
Anne Marie was into mermaids and horses.
Minna's more into cats, but
Minna will make do alone.
Minna's a composer!
Minna settles into her seat, thrilled about the ferry.
The Baltic is capricious.
The Baltic's deep and smooth.
The Baltic's a bowl, a submarine valley.
The Baltic's as balmy as a bathtub.
Minna's brought her bathing suit along.
It's late in August.
Minna's stoked.
Minna's heading away from what hurts.
No one's going to inflict any more damage, Minna thinks.
Everything's going to get sorted, Minna thinks, because
Minna wants to grow an asshole filter.

Minna thinks she can grow it quickly.
Minna's broken heart dwells in the breast of an optimist.

*

Minna's boarded the *Leonora Christine*.
The school camp's shepherded onto the upper deck.
The school camp's met another school camp.
The school camps exchange sexual fluids.
Minna drinks coffee in the stern canteen.
The canteen's full of retirees.
The retirees swarm up from the vehicle deck.
The retirees want to sit with one other.
Minna moves gladly.
Minna moves for two pairs of friends in their mid-seventies.
The gentlemen immediately order beer.
The missuses have newly permed hair.
The missuses make do with orange soda.
The gentlemen squeeze their permed missuses.
The missuses giggle.
The retirees have sex.
Minna can see that they have sex.
Minna thinks of Mom.
Minna dismisses the thought.
The thought lands on Lars.
Lars without clothes on.
Lars with a hard-on.
Minna on horseback.
Cat on a hot tin roof.
Minna and Lars, genital to genital, no respect.
Minna blushes on the plastic ferry seat.

Minna's been the fuck buddy of a disrespectful man.
That's the way it is, thinks Minna.
Minna's backbone withers.
Lars prefers sex with a machete.
It's unbearable, but there you have it.
The retirees raise their glasses.
Minna takes up Bergman from her pack.
The *Leonora Christine* pulls away from the quay.
The *Leonora Christine* heads out.
Minna glances down at Bergman.
Bergman says, *I pretend to be an adult.*
Bergman says, *Time and again it amazes me that people take me seriously.*
Minna loves Bergman.
Bergman lunges for Minna with the truth.
Bergman holds her tight, and now she glances at the door to the vehicle deck.
The door opens.
A small group of retirees trickles in.
Minna feels initially serene at the sight.
It doesn't last.
Minna raises Bergman to her face.
Minna slouches in her seat.
Minna wants to get off the *Leonora Christine.*
The *Leonora Christine* has set course for Rønne, but
Minna wants to leave.
Minna was once a music teacher at a folk high school.
Minna taught weeklong classes for happy amateurs.
The happy amateurs signed up in torrents.
The folk high school provided housing.

The folk high school was always going bust.
The amateurs had dough.
People stood there with guitars and piccolos.
People wanted to be virtuous.
Minna tried to teach them a bit of notation.
Minna clapped in time.
Minna played Bach for them.
Minna was trampled by dwarfs.
Minna ran out of options.
Minna let them sing from the tired Danish songbook.
The amateurs sang, *Is the light only for the learnèd?*
Minna had her own take.
The amateurs felt disgruntled about their rooms.
Minna found them new ones.
The amateurs lost their things:
Dentures, rollators, and spectacles vanishing every instant.
Prosthetic legs and large-print books: gone.
Grundtvig hovered above the waters.
Grundtvig illuminated the scene.
Grundtvig was high on sugar water and the life of
the mind.
Minna had to see to all the practicalities herself.
The amateurs loved Minna.
The amateurs pinched her on the cheek.
The amateurs wanted to sing at the farewell party.
The party was full of music that Minna had inflicted on
their world.
Minna wept.
Minna felt ashamed.
Minna needed rent.

Minna was keeping the wolf from the door, but
The wolf was preferable in the end.
Minna quit and is now en route to Bornholm.
Minna sits behind Bergman on the *Leonora Christine*.
Minna has recognized the hindmost retiree.
The retiree's named Gunvor Kramer.
Gunvor Kramer's a happy amateur.
Gunvor Kramer's a sincere person, but even worse:
Gunvor's on Facebook, and even worse:
Gunvor's convinced that she and Minna are colleagues.
Gunvor recorded a Christmas tape.
Gunvor recorded it on a reel-to-reel.
The reel-to-reel stands in Gunvor's living room.
Gunvor is thus a composer.
Gunvor writes Minna often.
Gunvor writes about her breakthroughs in the art of music,
    but even worse:
Gunvor Kramer's aboard the *Leonora Christine*.
Gunvor Kramer's set a course for Minna.
Minna knows that her holiday hangs by a thread.
Gunvor's in a car, you see.
Gunvor would like to chauffeur Minna around the island.
Gunvor would like to sing all her compositions for Minna,
    vibrato.
Minna presses Bergman to her face.
Gunvor passes by somewhere to the rear.
Gunvor walks slowly, slowly.
Minna turns cautiously.
Gunvor has sat down two booths away, with her back
    to Minna.

It's silly of course.
Gunvor's merely a person.
Gunvor loves #544 in the tired Danish songbook.
Gunvor loves chain dancing.
Gunvor has a droopy bosom.
Minna was dragged in as an unwilling witness.
Minna tucks Bergman into her backpack.
Minna rediscovers her sunglasses.
The sunglasses slip down in front of her face.
Gunvor's started on the candy catalogue.
Gunvor's found a ballpoint pen.
Gunvor sets checkmarks by candy.
The sunglasses shield Minna from Gunvor.
Minna passes Gunvor.
Minna's set a course for the stern.
Minna catches sight of the sea.
The Baltic lies blue and piercing.
The *Leonora Christine* shoves its way forward, self-confidence in its hull.
The *Leonora Christine* heads down the coast.
Minna slouches in a seat.
Minna hugs her backpack.
Minna oozes adrenaline.
Swedish customs opens for candy and liquor purchasers.
Swedish customs is full of retirees.
Gunvor forages.
Minna leans back.
No one heeds her anymore.
Minna's alone and can plan her escape.

*

Minna's arrived in Rønne.
Elisabeth's gotten a hold of her.
Mom's making plans for the weekend, but
Minna isn't home.
Elisabeth wants to know where she is, but
Minna's just not home.
Bornholm waits in the sunshine.
Bus #5 swoops across the island.
Minna's looking forward to seeing the landscape again.
Minna's quickly disappointed.
Bornholm had more cliffs in her memory.
Bornholm was exotic, Swedish.
Bornholm seems abandoned now.
The bus stop spots are dusty.
The butcher's closed.
The baker, the dairy, the school.
Bjarne's tanning salon has set up shop in the supermarket.
Bjarne's tanning salon browns the serfs.
Bjarne's tanning salon turns little girls into reality stars.
Bjarne makes a mint on the villages' decline.
The province assuages grief with porn.
The houses are cheap.
The houses have signs in their windows.
The houses are OPEN, OPEN, OPEN.
Most folks have fled.
Randiness remains.
Minna can see that a country is about to disappear.
Minna can see that the tracks point over the cliff edge.
Minna feels like a slum tourist.
That wasn't the idea with this holiday, thinks Minna.

Minna regards a shelter in Østerlars.
The round church has wandered off.
The round church has taken a room in Copenhagen.
Grief is latent in Minna.
Grief seizes its chance.
Minna gets moisture in her eyes.
Minna wipes the moisture away.
Minna wants to find a rock in the sea.
Minna wants to go out to the rock and sit.
Bergman will join her, and a thermos of coffee.
The cliffs begin someplace.
Minna googled Svaneke.
Minna saw the cliffs on the web.
The idyll will take over sooner or later.
Minna glances down in her backpack.
The cellphone sits down there.
Elisabeth's name throbs like an irate artery.
Minna shuts the pack.
Minna can see a large field of grain.
Minna can see a steep slope.
Bus #5 drives through the grain.
The sea appears at the foot of the hill.
The Baltic doubles over, vast and wet.
Bus #5 is headed toward Listed, and now it happens.
Bornholm opens up.
Bornholm looks like itself in the pictures.
The smokehouse has a flame under the herring.
Troll figurines have appeared in the windows.
The cliffs fall crumbling into the water.
The sea is blue-black, with swans in it.

The bus winds through charming houses.
The bus holds for a school camp.
The bus holds for another school camp.
The bus holds for a flock of retirees.
The bus swings gently down the coast and into Svaneke.
Minna presses the STOP button.
The bus stops by the hard-candy store.
Minna struggles with her wheeled suitcase, and then she's
standing there.
Minna stands there and is reminded of the Old Town in Aarhus.
Minna's reminded of the trips to Ballehage Beach.
Minna remembers her toes on the pier.
Minna with webbed feet.
Minna with piano fingers.
Minna with song in her throat.
Minna with a future before her, but
Elisabeth rings loudly in the pack.
Elisabeth's on Minna's trail.
Minna refuses to yield.
Minna fumbles in her pocket for the address.
Minna's going to live in a room with a tea kitchen.
The room has a view across the harbor.
The landlady's a friend of a friend.
Minna's not hoping that the landlady's gregarious.
Minna wants to be alone in the Baltic.
Minna stands quietly on the square.
Minna sees people everywhere.
The people are speaking Copenhagen dialect.
The people are looking for a ceramist.
Minna stands in the people's way.

Minna must make way.
Minna wheels her suitcase forward and back.
Minna's in the midst of a transport tsunami.

*

The lodgings in this case are not lacking.
Half-timbering goes with everything.
The foundation is Bornholm granite.
The room has a table, sofa, and bed.
The room isn't missing a thing, *au contraire*.
The room has latticed windows with geraniums.
Minna's rubbed the scented leaves between her fingers.
Minna's said hello to the landlady.
The landlady was in her mid-forties.
The landlady bore the mark of tourism.
Minna said that she had to quote *work during her stay*.
Minna's used that trick before.
People with projects are left in peace.
Minna has the one end of the house.
The door between Minna and the landlady is locked.
Nobody'll come barging in, the landlady promised.
That's great, and yet it isn't anyway.
The landlady's got a dog.
The dog bays.
The dog's bayed ever since the landlady left to do her shopping.
Minna sees the dog before her:
The dog's muzzle pointed skyward.
The dog's lower lip pushed forward.
The dog's eyes squinting ceilingward.

The dog doesn't want to be alone.
Minna's just the other side of the landlady's locked door.
The dog can hear Minna.
The dog doesn't understand that Minna can't rescue it.
Minna's hushed the dog through the keyhole.
Minna's acted as if she's gone to the grocery store.
The dog isn't fooled by cheap tricks.
The dog has nothing to do but complain about the program.
Minna puts her earplugs into action.
Minna sits in a soundproof bubble.
Minna can hear her breathing in the bubble.
Minna's lungs puff quietly.
Minna's pulse vibrates.
Minna closes her eyes and listens.
The ocean buzzes in Minna's veins.
The ocean calls from Minna's interior.
The ocean's outside the window, but
The ocean's inside Minna too.
Minna sits with the sea inside.
Minna ought to go for a walk, she knows.
Svaneke awaits outside and lovely.
People circle like good-natured sharks.
Minna should walk past them and out to a cliff, but
Minna's deaf and listens.
Minna's interior is a rehash of memories.
Minna paddles around in the old days.
Minna feels her body shifting.
Minna's senses are returning.
Hands down through the sand.
Hands up toward the gulls.

Dad's hand and Minna's.
The blue delta of Dad's hand.
The sea rises in Minna.
The sea finds fissures in Minna.
Minna's leaky.
Minna opens her eyes and blinks.
The sea trickles slowly.
The sea reaches land.
The beads of gravel rattle.
Minna blows her nose.
Minna should find herself a cliff.
Minna and Bergman should walk out onto the cliff and sit.
Minna shouldn't do anything else.
Minna thinks that Gunvor's peeping in the window.
The geraniums block the inward view.
Bornholm's relatively large.
The likelihood's small, but
Minna peeks out from behind a plant.
Svaneke harbor rocks with boats.
The tourists balance glass plates.
The tourists turn the corner in sensible shoes.
The tourists position themselves willingly in line.
The cliffs are out there.
The cliffs are warm from the day's sun.
Minna runs a hand across her face.
Minna opens her backpack.
Bergman's lying down there.
Dread makes the dreaded real, he repeats.
Minna nods.
Minna closes her eyes.

Minna whispers out into the lodgings: *Now the dog howls no more.*
The dog's done with playing forsaken.
The dog's shut its mouth.
The dog lies in its basket.
The dog begs for its ball.
The dog has nothing more to say about its situation.
Minna removes the earplug on the right side.
Minna listens with her head cocked.
—
The dog howls.
The dog howls skyward.

*

Minna's crawled out as far as she can go.
Minna sits on the blanket she brought.
The granite drills up gently into her buttock.
The gulls have set up camp on a couple cliffs farther out.
Christiansø is a seed on the horizon.
Christiansø beckons with its outpost nature.
Minna doesn't want to be any farther out now.
Minna just wants to sit here.
Minna wants to drink her coffee with Bergman.
The waves smack gently against the cliff.
The world smells of seaweed.
Minna sits and is doing fine.
Minna comes to think of Vagn.
Minna took a first-aid course of Vagn's.
Minna's never rescued anyone, but
Vagn knew all about hurt people.

Vagn said, *Hold their hand!*
Vagn said, *Bodily contact helps the injured!*
Vagn said, *Caresses and calm speech'll pass the time.*
The ambulance'll get there sooner or later.
A human being could use another human in the meantime.
A small hand is enough!
Minna looks around her circle of acquaintances.
The circle of acquaintances can't get a hand out through the shield.
The circle of acquaintances can't get skin on skin.
Minna considers her hand.
Minna doesn't need to play pious.
Minna's hand has withdrawn from the struggle.
Minna's hand hasn't touched anyone since Lars.
Lars was so real under the duvet.
Lars was so gentle down there.
Lars dared in the dark, but
The light demands trend awareness.
Minna's not trendy.
Minna's soft and warm every day.
The everyday doesn't cut it.
Minna takes her hand from the sea and sticks it in her mouth.
The sea tastes good.
The lighthouse towers behind her.
Årsdale nestles to the south.
Christiansø is Denmark's remotest enclave.
This rock's a rehearsal space, thinks Minna.
The gulls are the only ones present.
Minna can make noise the way she wishes.
Minna feels something slipping far below.

Minna's belly grows in capacity.
The lungs become bellows.
The throat a swan's.
The voice full of rust.
Minna's needed rehearsal space, but
Bornholm's big.
Bornholm has no objection if Minna warbles a trill.
The song has light, Minna sings.
Minna doesn't know where it's coming from, but it persists.
The song has warmth, she sings.
Minna recalls the folk high school now.
The song has eternity.
Minna thinks it's a strange song.
Minna sings the song anyway.
Minna's voice rises plumb upward.
The voice is like a beanpole.
Minna can climb it.
Minna can reach the stars.
Minna can reach the giant, the golden eggs, the empyrean.
Minna's good at climbing, but then she dives.
It does the voice good to plunge headlong.
The voice breaks the surface of the sea.
The voice continues toward the bottom.
The sea grass sways and tickles.
The marine fauna stands still and listens.
The voice is alone with itself and the wet.
Minna closes her eyes and she sings,
The song unites as it fades.
That's not enough for Minna.
Minna gives the song a last burst.

Minna's heart lifts.
The gulls rise.
The wings flutter.
The wings applaud and applaud.
Minna opens her eyes, and there stands an angler.
The angler stands on the rock ten yards away.
The angler looks at Minna.
The angler creaks in his rubber boots.
The angler calls out,
The fish are getting spooked.
Minna blushes: *I thought I was alone.*
A kayaker instantly paddles past.
Another kayaker, and yet another.
The kayakers paddle past like geese in a village pond.
The angler points somewhere behind Minna.
Minna turns around.
The evening sun is blinding, but there sit a man and a woman.
The man and woman wave with their cigarettes.
The woman says that it sounded lovely.
Minna repeats that she thought she was alone.
The woman and the man often sit by the lighthouse in
the evening.
The view of Christiansø, says the man.
The view of the bathers, says the woman.
The woman points at a springboard a little ways off.
People are leaping from the springboard down among the cliffs.
The campground tents sprout up among the brush.
Minna doesn't want to know anything else, but
The couple's from Østerbro in Copenhagen.
The couple could stay on Bornholm forever.

The woman pinches the man on the thigh.
The man pinches the woman on the thigh.
The man has large lips.
The woman isn't wearing a bra.
Minna wishes it weren't embarrassing to leave.
Bergman smiles at her from down on the granite.
Bergman declares that she's never been lovelier, but
Bergman would lie worse than a horse runs if his prick were
in a pickle.
Flight is a sign of weakness, she whispers.
Silence descends.
Silence is no longer a balm for the soul.
Silence is a social defect.
Minna feels the need to converse a bit.
Minna asks whether the couple has a cottage.
The woman says the cottage belongs to her husband.
The husband in question isn't along on holiday.
The man with the large lips on the other hand is along for
the whole trip.
The man asks Minna where she's from.
Minna doesn't know what to say.
Minna has more of an impulse to cry.
Aarhus—, says Minna.
Minna is suddenly unsure.
Minna felt at home in the song a few minutes ago.
The song disappeared, down toward the bottom.
The song stands still among the herring.
Everything else belongs to another reality.
Everything else, Minna thinks to herself, *is mere geography.*

*

Minna's crawled into bed at her lodgings.
The landlady's not home.
The dog's inconsolable.
Minna's stuffed a quilt around the bottom of the door.
Minna's glad she has earplugs.
Minna's glad she's by herself again.
The man and woman wanted to accompany her to Svaneke.
Minna was dragged in as an unwilling witness.
Minna didn't escape the couple till they were at the
harbor kiosk.
Disappointment inhabits her mind like rainy weather.
Minna really wants an asshole filter.
Minna wants to start setting limits.
Minna can't say yes or no, and
Minna's legs feel heavy.
The duvet feels strange.
The lodgings smell of cottage.
Minna thinks of spooks.
Minna's only afraid of spooks once in a while.
Minna doesn't believe in spooks, but
Things you don't believe in often exist anyway.
The Grauballe Man haunted Minna one spring when she
was a child.
The Grauballe Man lay dead in the Moesgaard Museum, but
The Grauballe Man walks around at night.
The Grauballe Man wriggles out of his display.
The Grauballe Man stands out on the cobblestones.
The Grauballe Man walks into Marselisborg Forest.
The Grauballe Man loves nature – and Minna.
The bog man in any case visits Minna at night.

Minna lies in her small bed with the duvet pulled up to her nose.
Minna lies and stares at the door of her room.
The living room resounds with the sound of coffee cups.
Elisabeth's room resounds with the sound of high-school boys.
Minna lies with her eyes on stalks, and then!
The door opens, and who should enter?
Minna's friend from Marselisborg Forest.
The Grauballe Man smells of harness.
The Grauballe Man's body is a story of its own.
The head crushed.
The throat cut.
The feet flat and lumpy, but what's worse:
The bog man leans over Minna.
The bog man's picked anemones for Minna.
The bog man boasts of his earthly remains.
The bog man still has flesh on his bones.
Minna will end up a skeleton!
Dad too!
Mom!
Elisabeth?
Minna doesn't believe in spooks.
Minna believes in the Grauballe Man.
Minna lies in her Bornholm sanctuary.
Minna considers the spiritual probabilities.
Bergman haunts her too.
Elisabeth employs demons.
The Fenris wolf howls.
The spooks are coming if they exist.
Elisabeth's coming if she discovers where Minna is.
Elisabeth wants to have the little ones under her thumb.

Minna just wants to love the little ones.
Minna's little ones would never lack for sweets.
Minna's little ones would grow roly-poly.
Minna really can't say no.
It doesn't matter now anyhow.
Minna won't become anyone's mother, and
Kids are the worst spooks in the world.
Kids can't understand that they don't exist.
Kids stick their cold hands under the duvet.
Kids would like to slap the sleeper's face.
Minna collects herself.
Minna forces herself to think of dull things.
Minna makes plans for the morrow.
Minna wants to go farther out.
Minna wants to find a rock so desolate.
Minna wants to go out to the rock and sing.
Minna wants to make sure she's alone.
Minna wants to stand there and get everything to swing.
The song will vault higher and higher.
The sky will stretch itself open,
The waves cast themselves against the cliff,
The ships beat into the wind.
Minna presses herself down into her rented linen.
Minna pushes herself out of reality.
The children exit Minna's consciousness.
The children go with the Grauballe Man.
Marselisborg Forest closes up after them.
The museum awaits.
The roe deer.

*

Minna's put on her bathing suit under her sundress.
Minna wants to go out and sing and get a tan.
Minna wants to rock-bathe.
Minna has to get provisions first.
Minna's gone for a walk in town.
Svaneke's lovely.
Svaneke's light yellow.
Svaneke's a set piece, thinks Minna.
The sky a stage border.
The smokehouse a sort of canteen.
The knickknack shops = the costume department.
Minna plays with the motif, and there's something to it.
Minna does like Svaneke, but
Svaneke reminds her a bit of Linda.
The houses have tricked themselves out for the season.
The houses bulge with whitewashed plinths.
Minna raises her eyes to the horizon.
The ocean's not going anywhere.
The ocean's seen much worse.
The cliffs are above thoughts of time.
The Baltic, Årsdale!
Minna wants to hike toward Årsdale a bit later.
Minna wants to hike so far south that she can hike in peace.
Minna's looked at the map.
The rocks extend a long way out down there.
The rocks permit clambering.
Minna can walk far out onto the rocks.
Minna's on her way down and out, but
Svaneke Dairy is famed for its beer ice cream.
Svaneke Dairy lies en route.

Minna wants to have an ice cream to hike on.
The weather's good for ice cream, and lots of people have thought the same thing:
The tourists have formed a line.
The line reaches far out into the gravel.
The line hardly budges.
The small children crawl around on a plastic cow in the courtyard.
The mothers stand in line.
The fathers look after the kids.
The retirees rummage in their purses.
The retirees cannot find their spectacles.
The waitresses are dressed in Morten Korch costumes.
The waitresses resemble actresses from the Fifties.
The waitresses look like Tove Maës and Ghita Nørby.
The waitresses hobble becomingly in their feudal shoes.
The waitresses look homespun by the latte machines.
Minna's crept forward a little ways in the line now.
Minna can see that there are celebrities in the line.
The celebrities take a long time to serve.
The retirees are on a first-name basis with the celebrities.
The small children ride the cow.
The fathers look at smartphones.
The mothers are ready to crack.
Minna on the other hand is of good cheer.
Minna wants to have a cup of coffee with her ice cream.
Minna's advanced far in the line.
Minna's about to order.
Tove Maës just can't see Minna.
Tove Maës can only see the celebrity.

The celebrity's from on TV.
The celebrity will have ice cream with licorice in it.
The celebrity will have espresso.
The celebrity flaunts the fact that he comes here often.
Tove Maës and the celebrity gossip about the locals.
Ghita Nørby limps out for more sherbet.
Ghita and Tove want to serve the celebrity best.
The celebrity can get what he wants.
Minna's been cut in front of twice now.
Minna raises her hand tentatively.
Minna gets up on tiptoe.
The celebrity laughs loud and long.
Tove Maës laughs loud and long.
The retirees' hip cement begins to crumble.
The kids will be confirmed soon.
The mothers and fathers have long since been divorced.
Minna says, *Excuse me!*
Minna's surprised to hear her own voice.
Minna continues, *There are lots of folks who're waiting.*
Tove Maës freezes under her bonnet.
Ghita Nørby moves in frames.
Minna blushes with justice on her side.
Minna orders a caffe latte.
Minna orders a tub of beer ice cream.
Tove Maës hobbles over to the coffee machine.
Ghita Nørby shoots the celebrity a glance.
The celebrity walks out into the courtyard.
The retiree behind Minna smiles gratefully.
Minna looks proudly back at the line.
Minna regards the people she's rescued.

Minna's proud of her sudden asshole filter.
Minna sticks a feather in her cap.
Small victories count too, she thinks.
A hand pokes up in the middle of the line.
The hand pokes up and waves.
A large gray head pops to the side.
Gunvor's mouth is a gaping O.
Gunvor calls out Minna's name loudly in the dairy.
Minna! It's me! Gunvor Kramer! From the folk high school!
Minna hears her coffee fizz out of the coffee machine.
Tove Maës sends a wicked smile out of the corner of her mouth.
Minna's asshole filter worked well two seconds ago, but
Minna's asshole filter has large holes in the mesh.

*

Gunvor Kramer's found a corner in the courtyard.
Gunvor Kramer's pushed Minna deep into the corner.
Gunvor Kramer's wearing a linen smock.
Gunvor Kramer's hair is pinned fast with a Viking clasp.
Gunvor's been thinking a lot about Minna.
Minna's made a big difference for Gunvor.
Gunvor was only capable of simple compositions.
Gunvor couldn't get larger works to hang together.
Gunvor mostly preferred music with a chorus.
Gunvor was stuck artistically.
Minna helped her advance.
Gunvor stands in the supermarket, and then it happens.
Gunvor has to run out of the store.
Gunvor has to go over to her car.
Gunvor seats herself behind the wheel.

Gunvor finds her notebook in her purse.
Gunvor writes down the lyrics.
Gunvor hums the melody.
This is just an example, says Gunvor.
Gunvor clears her throat.
Minna's coffee halts in front of her mouth.
The coffee steams in the morning heat.
The beer ice cream melts.
Gunvor sings a song.
The song's about love.
Love is vulnerable, sings Gunvor.
Love falls to pieces so easy, she sings.
People are so busy.
No one should forget anyone.
No one should forget anyone.
Gunvor's eyes are large and shiny.
Gunvor's finished now.
Gunvor says that it's the prologue to a cantata.
The cantata's still missing a lot.
Minna smiles and grasps her beer ice cream.
Minna moves over on the bench.
Minna says, *It's nice to know you got something out of the class.*
Gunvor scrapes the bottom of her sherbet tub.
Gunvor asks how long Minna's going to be on Bornholm.
Minna answers vaguely.
Gunvor gets an idea.
Gunvor's planned a day trip to Dueodde.
It's hot, Gunvor says, *let's go down and bathe.*
Minna says, *I'm not big on swimming.*
Gunvor points at her sundress and asks, *Why the bathing suit?*

Minna needn't reply.
Minna doesn't owe Gunvor a reply.
Gunvor's already moved on anyhow.
Gunvor tells her about the sand in Dueodde.
The sand is fine.
The sand gets into every fold of skin.
Gunvor slaps her thighs.
The skinfolds quiver.
Something moves inside the linen smock.
Minna feels powerless, especially in her face.
Minna needs to put up a fight.
Minna's mouth tries to come up with a lie.
Minna's mouth doesn't want to say anything.
Gunvor's mouth doesn't want anything but, but now Minna gets lucky:
The backpack rings.
Minna's backpack is sitting on the bench and ringing.
Gunvor looks at the backpack.
Minna knows quite well who's hiding in the pack.
Minna opens it up anyway.
People ought to go away when they talk on their cells.
Anything else is rude.
Minna presses the answer button.
Minna gets up carefully from the bench.
Minna leaves the corner with Gunvor.
Minna here.
It's about time! says Elisabeth.
Elisabeth gets down to business.
Elisabeth's been saving up.
Minna walks hesitantly through the courtyard.

Minna approaches the cow.
Elisabeth pricks up her ears on the other end.
Elisabeth asks, *Who are those kids?*
Minna says, *I don't know.*
That's true enough, but not true enough for the sister.
Elisabeth says that it's hard to be related to Minna.
Elisabeth says that it's getting harder and harder.
Elisabeth says that Mom and Finn are coming for the weekend.
Mom and Finn can't stay in Potato Row.
The bench isn't for sitting on, she says.
Elisabeth says that if Minna went to Aarhus more often.
Elisabeth says that it'd never happen if . . .
Minna's rounded the corner of the dairy.
Svaneke harbor lies before her.
The boats rock in the late summer breeze.
Gunvor sits in the courtyard.
Minna has her backpack with her.
Minna's sandals have non-slip soles.
Nothing's to prevent her.
The path is clear.
Who's going to stop her?
The sister wants to know where Minna is, and
Minna's running.
Minna's running down to the harbor.
Minna's on her way south, away from Svaneke.
Elisabeth says, *Answer me! Where?*
Minna says, *I'm on my way to Årsdale.*
Elisabeth doesn't know where Årsdale is.
Årsdale's in North Jutland, Minna says.
Årsdale's a little place south of Aalborg.

Everyone knows that, Minna says.
Minna can hear that Elisabeth didn't know that.
Minna can hear her sister's disbelief, but
Minna's positive, and now the connection's breaking up.
The connection crackles and hisses.
The connection gets so bad that Minna disappears.
Minna disappears.
Minna's feet take wing.
Minna's an instance of female buoyancy and helium.

*

The rock's flat and sloping.
The rock's wet at the base.
The sun hangs heavy as a plum.
The sea's blue-black.
Minna's seen it:
The Bay of Aarhus is a fresh blue plain.
The Sound's a bottle-green river, but
The Baltic's black and greasy.
Minna's taken off her sundress.
Minna's smeared herself with SPF 20.
Minna stands with her toes so that they get wet.
Minna wants to rock-bathe, but
The sea grass waves under the surface.
The bladderwrack has lashed itself fast.
The rock looks like a woman's sex under the surface.
Minna isn't really sure and glances behind her.
Minna had to clamber to get here.
Minna had to crawl and injure herself.
Minna had to rest en route.

Minna was in flight of course, but
Minna isn't thinking about Gunvor anymore.
Minna stares at the sea.
Minna sees the darkness shift downwards.
The darkness is deep on deep.
The loneliness profound.
Minna's got plenty of time.
Minna doesn't have to throw herself in.
The sky's vaulting.
The clouds assume their positions.
Minna's belly swells.
Something trickles.
Something else slides.
Minna lays her hands upon her midriff.
Minna inhales deep into her lungs.
Minna tilts back her neck.
Minna makes her mouth round, and then it arrives:
Minna sings a song in Latin.
Minna sings it with all that should've been.
Minna doesn't pull her punches:
Sed eligo quod video
Collum iugo prebeo;
Ad iugum tamen
Suave suave transeo.
The song feels like an incantation.
Latin has a menacing effect.
The words are like holy water.
The pelvis swaying.
The arms floating.
The feet stomping.

Minna chanting.
The sea licking her toes.
The song begins anew.
The song presses its way out again and again.
Minna senses the water's presence at her feet.
Minna thinks it's just grand getting cold feet.
Minna raises her voice as loud as it'll go.
The voice'll go very loud.
The voice can go maybe just loud enough too.
Minna wants to take a step backward.
The rock is slippery.
Minna's foot slips.
Minna slips with it.
Minna's legs rail against the sky.
Minna's head plunges toward stone.
Minna lands badly on her skull.
The skull breaks the fall of an entire woman.
Minna slides down into the water.
Minna slides down through the seaweed.
Minna sinks like a stone.
Minna's arms plow the water.
Minna's eyes are open and alive.
Minna's mouth is moist and round.
The sea feels like sweet chill.
The Baltic is a bowl.
The Baltic's a submarine valley.
Beauty won't deny itself.
The fish scoot off in gleaming procession.
The fish turn and pivot for Minna.
The scales glitter.

The eyes shine silver.
Minna reverts downward.
Minna wriggles her arms.
Minna waves to the darkness.
The darkness waves back.
Minna sees a gestalt in the darkness.
The gestalt has a beard.
The gestalt's mouth is a soft wet brushstroke.
Chest hair forces its way upward.
The beard wanders downward away from its chin.
An Adam's apple lies in the middle of the hair.
Dad? Minna thinks.
Dad waves.
Dad takes hold of Minna.
The fauna closes around them.
Bubbles seep from nose and mouth.
Hair flutters like sea grass.
Minna's pelvis has never been so round.
Minna's legs fuse and articulate.
Dad smiles at Minna.
Dad swims around Minna.
Minna says, *Helgenæs?*
Minna gets water in her mouth.
Minna gets a lot of water in her mouth.
Minna's lungs squeeze.
The lungs stretch.
The lungs are hard as cement.
The lungs don't want anything but to go upward.
Minna could happily continue downward, but
Minna's lungs want to go up.

Minna's bruised skull like a cork.
Minna's skull directional.
Minna's arms wretched fins.
Minna's legs kick and thrash.
The legs strike bedrock.
Minna's hands strike granite.
The rocks close around Minna.
Minna grasps the seaweed strands.
Minna grabs hold of Bornholm from below.
Minna throws up her arms in late-summerness.
Minna scrabbles on stone.
Minna searches for a chink.
Minna contracts like a muscle before it explodes.
Minna clings to dry land, angry and insecure.
Minna's tongue feels cold as bronze.
The sun acting up.
The corneas drying out.
Minna hauls herself farther up, and then she lies there.
Minna has rock-bathed.
Minna's been down and out.
Minna's toes plash in the surface of the ocean.
The rest of Minna has been decently salvaged.
Minna's world stands still.
Minna thinks of Dad in the water.
Minna thinks of her head.
Minna's head was apparently injured a bit.
The head hurting.
The mouth spitting.
Snot running.
The sun and the gulls having a look-see.

Minna lies with eyes shut.
Minna lies and listens.
Something rustles.
Minna raises her eyes, and there stand a pair of rubber shoes.
The shoes sit on a pair of feet.
The shoes shuffle uncertainly.
Hair pokes well out from the ankles.
A man has come to Minna's rescue.
Minna can't be bothered.
Minna's not going to be rescued now.
Minna's rescued herself.
Minna props herself up on an elbow: *Yes?*
The man asks, *Are you okay?*
Minna says, *I've been in the water.*
The man hunkers down: *On purpose?*
Minna says, *Not completely.*
The man wants to know if he should call for an ambulance.
Minna places her hands on the rock.
Minna raises herself a bit to sit.
Minna can see the man better now.
The man's plump.
The man has a beard.
Medium height.
The face attractive, and the mouth now opening.
The man says he could hear someone singing.
The man says he crawled out to have a look.
The man's got a banjo on his back.
Minna points at the banjo.
The man looks at the banjo as if it weren't his.
The banjo's his.

The banjo and he were on their way to Årsdale.
The man plays banjo during the tourist season.
Guitar's more for the mainland.
The man introduces himself.
The man says his name's Tim.
Tim seats himself at Minna's side.
Tim sets the banjo up against Minna's backpack.
Tim takes hold of Minna's hand.
Minna's hand is wet and cold.
Tim squeezes the hand a little.
The ambulance isn't out of the picture.
The medicopter isn't either.
Tim raises his index finger.
Tim says Minna should follow it with her eyes.
Tim's finger oscillates, but
Minna has her eye on something else.
The penny's dropped:
Tim's on Bornholm.
Tim's the cousin.
Tim knows someone with a rehearsal space in Kastrup.
The rehearsal space is cheap.
Minna can't stop looking.
Tim's family resemblance seeps out.
Tim does look like Lars.
Tim's beard is just more modest.
Tim also looks gentler.
Tim seems nice.
Tim's just about sweet.
Tim is Lars, like Lars was at night.
Tim is Lars without deadlines and Linda.

Lars was a porcupine.
Lars was a pillbox.
Tim's warm and hairy.
Tim's soft and shy.
Tim looks at her worriedly.
Tim says that she's bleeding from her head.
Minna says, *Who isn't?*
Tim says she's freezing, but
Minna isn't freezing.
It was me who sang, says Minna
    and then she shoots, she shoots him the mermaid eye.

QUOTATIONS IN THE TEXT

p. 13 The quotation is a slight paraphrase of "I drill, and either the drill breaks, or else I don't dare drill deep enough", from Ingmar Bergman, *Billeder* (*Images*, Copenhagen: Lindhardt og Ringhof, 1990). All quotations from Bergman have been rendered into English by Misha Hoekstra from Danish translations of the original Swedish texts.

p. 17 "Pointlessness grimaces!" in Bergman's *Laterna Magica* (*Magic Lantern*, Copenhagen: Lindhardt og Ringhof, 1987).

pp. 22–3 and 66 See Jens Peter Jacobsen's 1874 poem 'Arabesk: Til en Haandtegning af Michel Angelo' ('Arabesque: For a Drawing by Michelangelo'), which begins:

> Did the wave reach land?
> Did it reach land and trickle down slowly,
> Rattling with beads of gravel,
> Back once more into the world of waves?

(Translated from the Danish)

p. 30 Slight simplification of "The ringmaster of a flea circus, as you know, lets the artists suck his blood", from *Billeder*.

p. 30 "But a daydreamer isn't an artist except in his dreams", from *Billeder*.

p. 30 "I contain too much humanity" is the last part of "Here, in my solitude, I have an odd sense that I contain too much humanity", from *Billeder*.

p. 30 "The days are long, large, light. They're as substantial as cows, as some sort of bloody big animal", from *Billeder*.

p. 40 "You will do what is needed; when nothing is needed, you can't do anything", from *Billeder*.

p. 40 "Failures can have a fresh, bitter taste; the adversity rouses aggression and shakes slumbering creativity awake", from Ingmar Bergman, *Laterna Magica*.

pp. 55 and 66 "Dread makes the dreaded real" is adapted from Bergman's *Laterna Magica,* where it appears as "Dread would soon make the dreaded real".

p. 57 "I pretend to be an adult. Time and again it amazes me that people take me seriously", from *Billeder*.

p. 69 Minna sings Bjørnstjerne Bjørnson's 'Sangen Har Lysning' ('The Song Has Light'), also known as #159 in *Højskolesangbogen* (*The Danish Folk High School Songbook*).

p. 83 Minna sings the last stanza of Carl Orff's 'In Trutina' ('In the Balance'), whose lyric comes from a medieval manuscript. One rendering from the Latin (translator unknown):

> But I choose what I see
> And submit my neck to the yoke:
> I yield to the sweet, sweet yoke.

Also published by **PUSHKIN PRESS**